My first tunnel!

Me and Spider

The family holiday –
on Compost Island

For "the boys"–
Ken, Sean, Ryan, Patrick and Timothy
–D.C.

For Rozzie and Cheetah
–H.B.

Text copyright © 2003 by Doreen Cronin.
Illustrations copyright © 2003 by Harry Bliss.

First published in the US in 2003 by Joanna Cotler Books, an imprint of HarperCollins Publishers.
First published in paperback in the UK in 2012 by HarperCollins Children's Books.
HarperCollins Children's Books is a division of HarperCollins Publishers Ltd,
77-85 Fulham Palace Road, London W6 8JB

1 3 5 7 9 10 8 6 4 2

ISBN: 978-0-00-745590-4

DIARY OF A WORM

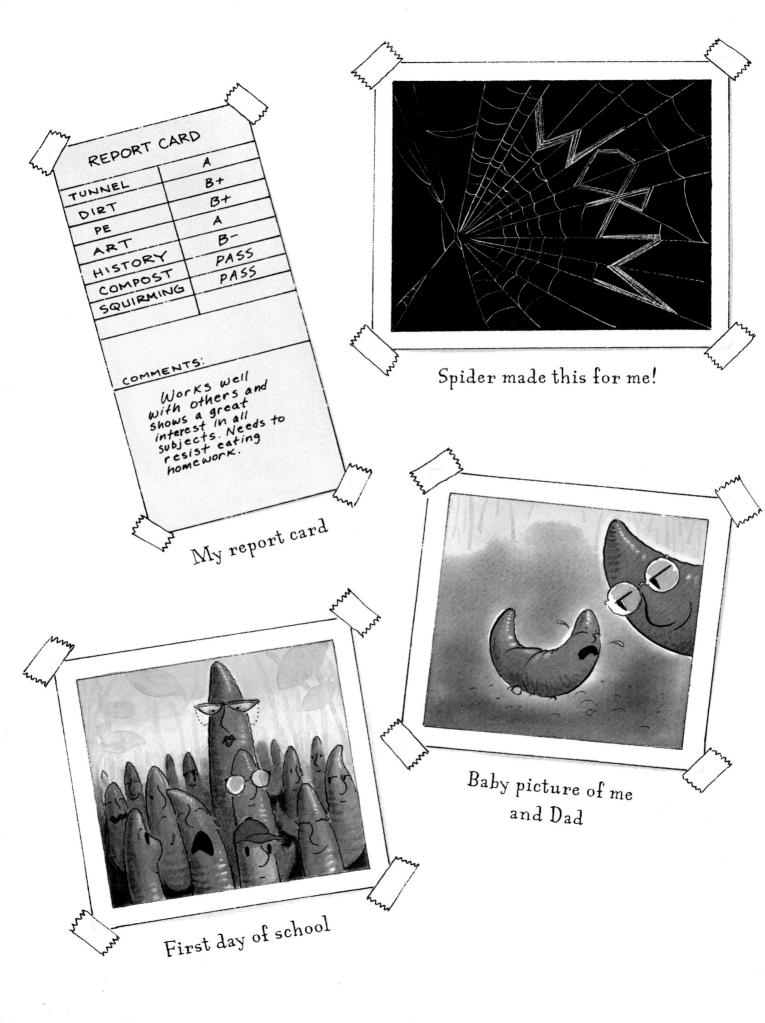

REPORT CARD

	A
TUNNEL	B+
DIRT	B+
PE	A
ART	B-
HISTORY	PASS
COMPOST	PASS
SQUIRMING	

COMMENTS:
Works well with others and shows a great interest in all subjects. Needs to resist eating homework.

My report card

Spider made this for me!

Baby picture of me and Dad

First day of school

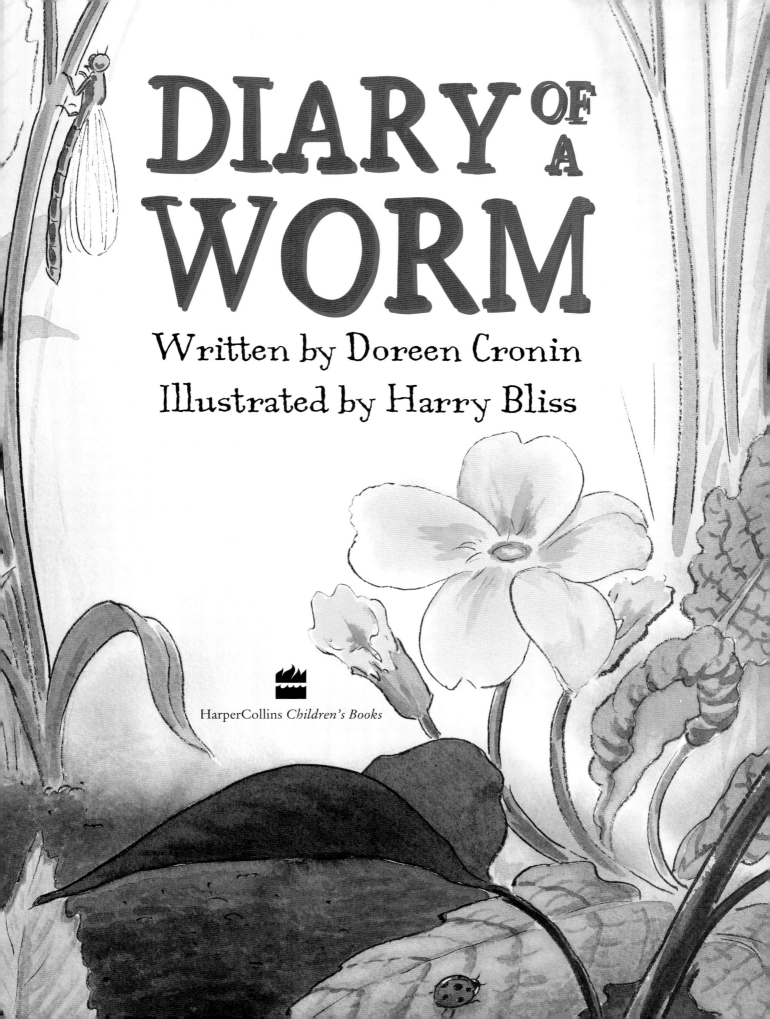

DIARY OF A WORM

Written by Doreen Cronin

Illustrated by Harry Bliss

HarperCollins *Children's Books*

MARCH 20

Mum says there are three things I should always remember:

1. The earth gives us everything we need.

2. When we dig tunnels, we help to take care of the earth.

3. Never bother Dad when he's eating the newspaper.

First all of his legs got stuck.

Then he swallowed a load of dirt.

Tomorrow he's going to teach
me how to walk upside down.

MARCH 30
Worms cannot walk upside down.

APRIL 10

It rained all night and the ground was soaked. We spent the entire day on the pavement.

Hopscotch is a very dangerous game.

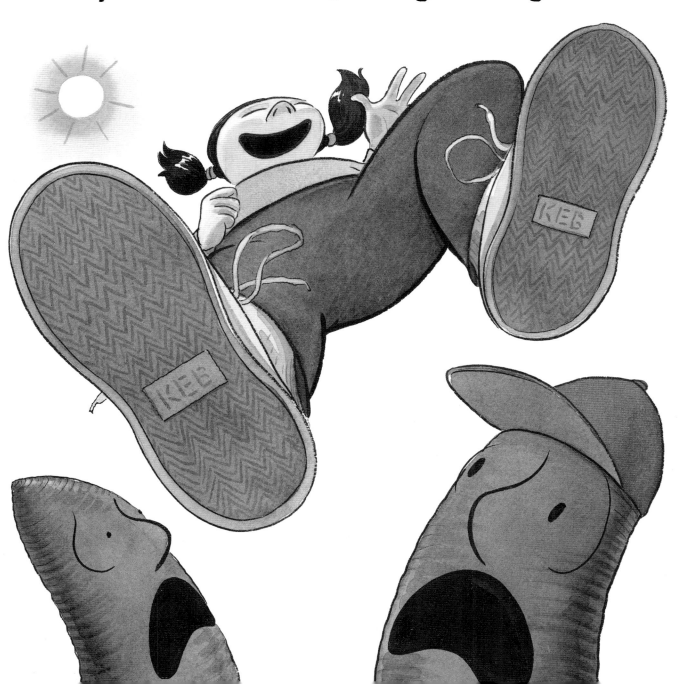

APRIL 15

I forgot my lunch today. I got so hungry that I ate my homework.

My teacher made me write "I will not eat my homework" ten times.

When I was finished, I ate that, too.

APRIL 20

I crept up on some kids in the park today. They didn't hear me coming.

I wiggled up right between them and they SCREAMED.

I love it when they do that.

Grandpa taught us that good manners are very important.

So today I said "good morning" to the first ant I saw.

MAY 8

Had the worst nightmare
last night —

giant birds playing hopscotch.

Mum says I have to stop eating so much rubbish right before I go to bed.

I got into a fight with Spider today.
He told me you need legs to be cool.
Then he ran. I couldn't keep up.
Maybe he's right.

MAY 16

I made Spider laugh so hard,
he fell out of his tree.
Who needs legs?

MAY 28

Last night I went to the school dance.

You put your head in.

You put your head out.

You do the hokey cokey
and you turn around.

That's all we could do.

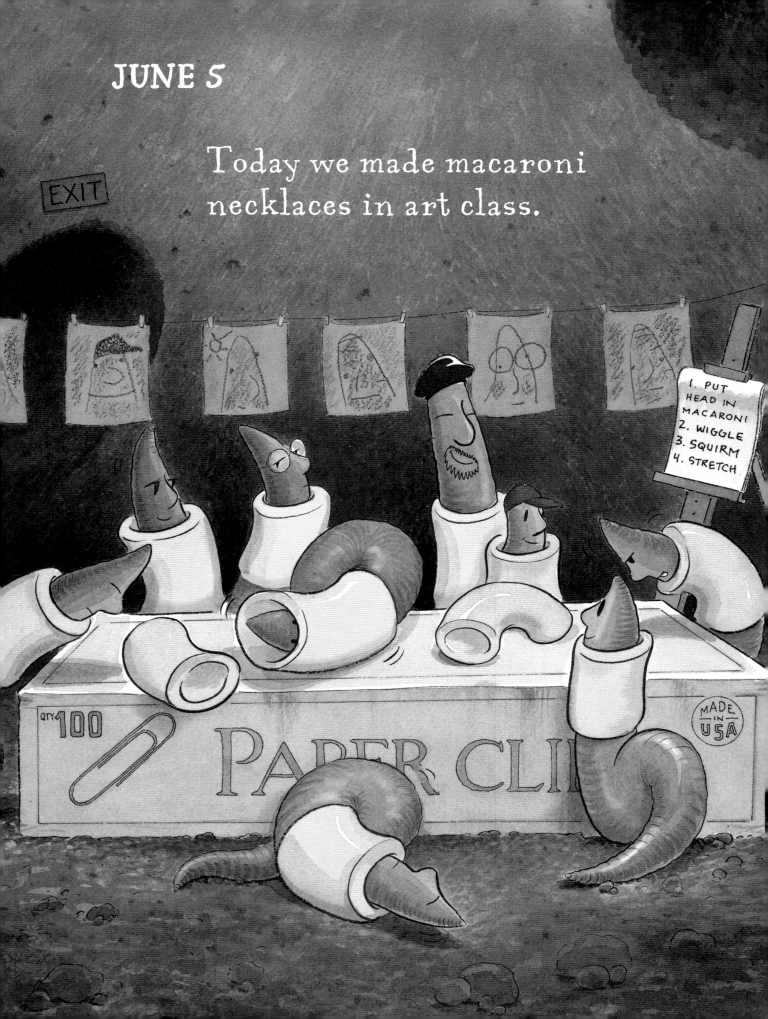

I brought mine home and
we ate it for dinner.

JUNE 15

My older sister thinks she's so pretty. I told her that no matter how much time she spends looking in the mirror, her face will always look just like her rear end.

Spider thought that
was really funny.

Mum did not.

When I grow up, I want to be a Secret Service agent. Spider says I will have to be very careful because the prime minister might step on me by mistake.

JULY 28

Three things I don't like about being a worm:

1. I can't chew gum.

2. I can't have a dog.

3. All that homework.

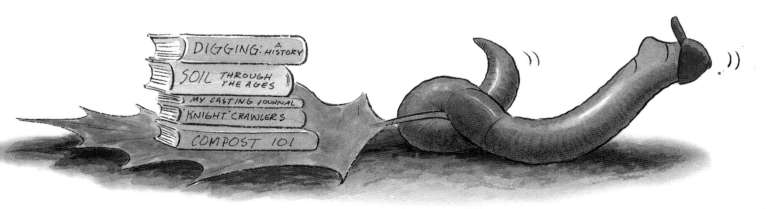

Three good things about being a worm:

1. I never have to go to the dentist.

2. I never get in trouble for trailing mud through the house.

3. I never have to take a bath.

AUGUST 1

It's not always easy being a worm. We're very small and sometimes people forget that we're even here.

But, like Mum always says, the earth never forgets we're here.

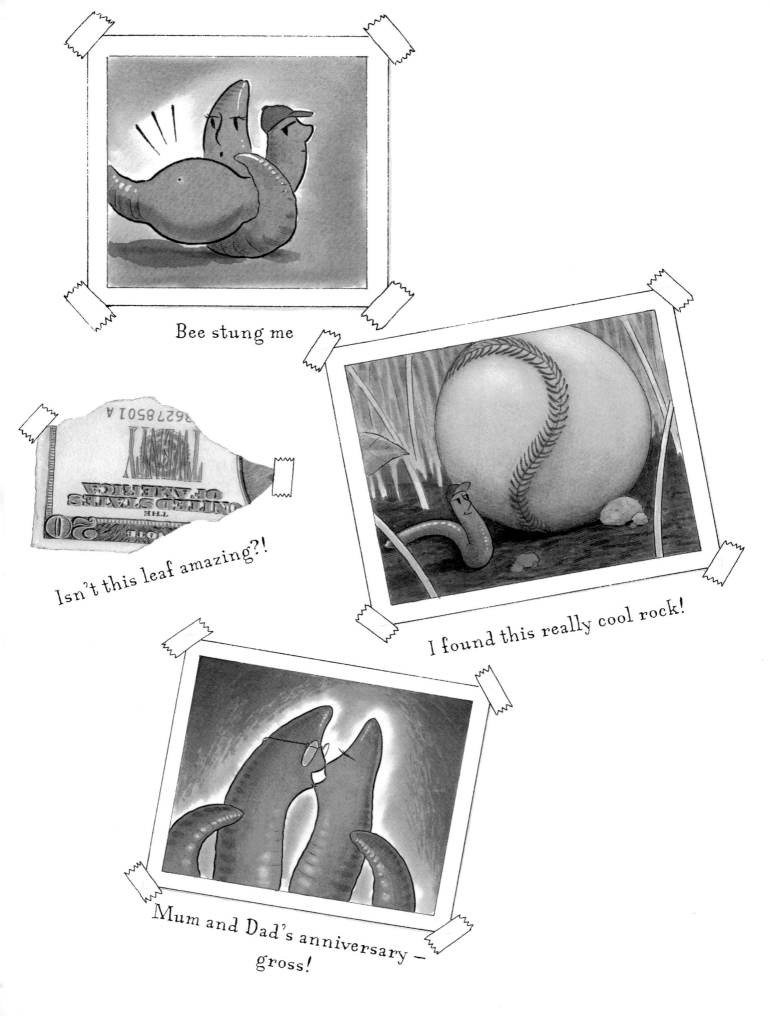

Bee stung me

Isn't this leaf amazing?!

I found this really cool rock!

Mum and Dad's anniversary — gross!

My own comic!

My sister's sleepover party
(hee, hee)

My favourite pile of dirt